A Cat Called Hop

By Oliver Clarke

Copyright 2013 Oliver Clarke

Cover photographs copyright 2013 Lisa Funk

To Kat,

In loving remembrance of all your beloved kittykats

All the very best,

For my wife, Angela, who continues to inspire, nurture and put up with me.

Contents

A Cat Called Hope 5

A Cat Called Hope Returns 32

A Cat Called Hope – The Final Chapter 59

Eulogy..89

A Note from the Author 93

A Cat Called Hope

Marx was his name. Not his real name obviously, just the name the humans used. He lived with two of them. Two female humans who brought him food and stroked him when he let them. They had their own names for each other but he called them the Walking and Sleeping. He called them that quite simply because one of them slept much of the time and the other ran around a lot. He wasn't sure why Sleeping did as much sleeping as she did. If it was because she was ill or if she just appreciated the benefit of sleep. Maybe she was part feline.

Marx had observed with interest the little humans who appeared on the moving picture screen that Walking and Sleeping had. The little ones didn't seem to sleep nearly as much as the one or walk quite as enthusiastically as the other so Marx suspected that the ladies he lived with might represent the extremes of human behaviour. It didn't really matter. They just were what they were.

The screen intrigued him, although not as much as it seemed to fascinate them. It was a little like a pool of water that he could see himself in only he saw the little humans instead. Sometimes there were no little humans and the screen was just black. At those times Marx could see himself and in many ways he preferred that.

So the three of them lived together. Sleeping did a lot of sleeping and Walking did a lot of walking and Marx did a bit of both. Walking was the only one who ever went outside. Marx and Sleeping would both sit by the window, sometimes together and sometimes not, and watch the world go by. Neither of them ever ventured out though. Marx would have quite liked to but they kept the doors and windows shut so he couldn't. As for Sleeping, he suspected it just wasn't really her thing.

And then one day it all changed.

Marx smelled it first. He was dozing on the window sill in the front room, watching the birds in the garden through one half opened eye. The scent reached his sensitive nostrils and brought him fully alert. It wasn't a smell he knew, although it was like the smell that Walking sometimes made when she was preparing food. His ears pricked up and he heard a crackling sound. It seemed to be coming from the same direction as the smell.

Marx got up and lazily stretched and decided to investigate. He padded across the room to the hallway and poked his head out into it. It was all coming from the room at the end, the one with the cold floor where he went to eat. As he walked towards it he felt the heat. Not warmth. Heat. He stopped. The smell was stronger now. Overpowering, blotting out everything else. The noise was louder too and increasing in volume by the second. Marx didn't know why but something inside him told him to run.

Much of the time he lived happily enough with the humans but every so often something clicked inside him. Something that reminded him that he wasn't supposed to live like this. Sometimes it happened when he was watching the birds in the garden, lazily watching them for want of anything better to do and then suddenly wondering what it would be like to feel their hot blood pumping into his mouth.

This was different though, because now he wasn't feeling excited. Now he was feeling scared. All his instincts were telling him to get as far away from the smell and the heat and the crackle as he could. Marx backed away from it, watching the door in case something sprang out of it at him. When he judged he was far enough from the danger he lithely turned and ran. The farthest point he knew from the heat was the room that Sleeping slept in so that's where he went, bounding up the stairs as quickly as he could. The door to her room was ajar and when he forcefully nudged it open it woke her up. She sat up with some effort and started to say something in her usual tired but comforting tone. Then he saw her nose twitch and her eyes go wide.

He'd never seen Sleeping move fast but she did now. Swinging her legs out of bed and reaching for that thing beside her bed that she spoke into. She started talking into it, quickly and nervously, her usual calmness gone. Marx jumped up onto the bed next to her and nuzzled her. He wanted to cheer her up but she just pushed him away. He backed up staring at her. She'd never done that before. Walking had, when she was bustling around doing things, but never Sleeping.

She stopped talking and stood up. Her legs were shaky beneath her but she looked determined. Marx was surprised when she called to him, putting her hand out to stroke him. He went to her and she grabbed him, sweeping him up into her arms and holding him tight. He thought about jumping down but decided to stay with her. It was nice to be held, especially after the fright he'd experienced downstairs. Well, not fright, he thought now, sensible concern.

Sleeping said soothing things to him and hugged him tight as she walked with difficulty across the room. Marx snuggled into her trying to find the few soft spots on her bony frame. She leaned down and kissed the top of his head. Then she threw him out of the open window.

The feeling was like nothing he'd experienced before. He'd jumped in the past, of course he'd jumped, but this was different. When he jumped it was his choice, he was in control. Now he had no control at all. His legs thrashed about under him desperately trying to gain purchase on something. There was nothing though, just air. The ground was getting closer, racing up towards him. Instinct took over. That thing deep inside him that reared up every so often. His brain was panicking but his body just relaxed. He landed softly, easily, his loose legs absorbing the impact.

He was outside. Not in the house but in the world he had seen through the windows. The green ground beneath his feet was cool, springy. He bent and sniffed it, taking in the fresh clean taste, then opened his mouth to bite one of the tempting little blades. He chewed it thoughtfully as he looked around. He wasn't sure if he should be frightened or excited. Everything was alien to him but his heart told him this was where he was meant to be. And then there was a great roaring and a whooping noise that made his ears go flat. He'd heard similar noises coming from the screen the humans watched but never this loud. He turned and saw a huge red something coming towards him. Massive, noisy, angry, thundering ever closer.

In a flash he had turned and run. His legs carrying him as fast as they could and further than they ever had before. His heart was pumping with fear but with exhilaration too. This felt good. Running felt good. Being free.

He left the house and the red beast behind him and headed towards the small stand of trees he'd gazed at so many times. He didn't know what they were but he knew he wanted to walk amongst them. Smell them, claw at them, sleep underneath them. The ground under his feet changed from the cool and soft to hard and warm and scratchy. He kept running, eyes on the trees, the red beast still roaring behind him. There was a screeching and a hissing and he looked back and saw that it had stopped. It came to a shuddering halt in front of the house and its sides moved in an unnatural way. Humans climbed out of it. Marx stopped. What on earth was it? Not a living thing. Not a beast. A human thing. One of the things they used to make their lives easier. Then Marx looked beyond it and saw the house. He could hear the crackle again now that the roaring had stopped. He could smell the harsh smell too. The difference now was that he could see it too, see a magical orange light flickering from the open window that Sleeping had thrown him out of. He stood there for a moment watching it, mesmerised, until a tremendous bang filled the air. He turned and ran again as the orange light engulfed the whole house.

He ran until he couldn't run anymore, through the trees, forgetting his dreams of playing amongst them, and out the other side. There was more of the scratchy black stuff there and he ran along that too. At first he ran to get away from the noise and then he did it because it felt good. It felt like what his long, loose legs had been made for. The running gave him something to focus on too; the concentration needed to dodge obstacles as they came at him blotted everything else out of his mind. It stopped him from thinking about Sleeping. About what she'd done. About what the bang meant.

When he stopped the sky was getting dark and his mouth and throat were so dry they hurt. His legs couldn't run any further and his paws were rubbed raw from the hard black ground.

He found a pool of water, on the road and drank from it. It was gritty, dull. Not at all like the sweet water or rich milk he was used to, but it quenched his thirst.

When he had finished drinking and his belly was full of it he looked around him for somewhere to sleep. He was on a long patch of hard grey ground with the backs of houses along one side. On the other side were what looked like little houses with no windows and big metal doors. One of those doors was open at the bottom (why did they open at the bottom not the side?) and he crept inside it. It was filled with dirty. smelly people things, all of them hard and uncomfortable looking. He managed to find an old blanket; rough like the one that Sleeping put over her legs if she sat downstairs. It stank of something foul but it was better than nothing. He padded it with his paws until it felt right and then lay down on it and closed his eyes. He started to think about Sleeping and the way she had dropped him from the window. Had that been to get him away from the heat? And then he thought about Walking. Where had she been? Out maybe, she came and she went and he didn't try to keep track of her. He pictured their pink faces, Walking's round and Sleeping's sharp, and then he fell asleep.

There was a little person prodding him when he woke up. Or rather a little person prodded him awake. She wasn't little like the people on the moving pictures screen, just smaller than Walking and Sleeping. She was smoother too.

Her little hand poked him again and she said something in a voice that was much quieter than even Sleeping's.

He stared back at her but did nothing. She didn't seem like a threat but he was still wary of her. It wasn't a question of trust, he'd never trusted any human. What was important was knowing enough about them to gauge how much quicker he was than them. Once he knew that he was comfortable. This little one didn't look that quick, she moved in a clumsy kind of a way, like she wasn't fully used to her body. He knew he could get away from her if he had to so he decided to wait and see what she would do. Now that he was awake he realised how hungry he was. She might give him food like Walking and Sleeping did. He hoped she would.

The girl stroked his back and he let her, pushing up against her. It felt good to be touched. Reassuring. He hadn't had time to think about what had happened, he'd been too busy running and then too tired. He realised now that he'd missed the touch of a human. He meowed at the girl, knowing she wouldn't understand exactly what he meant but hoping she would know he was being friendly. Her mouth turned up at the corners and she showed him her teeth. He'd learned over the years that this meant she was happy, even though it didn't look like that.

She said something back and stroked his head. Then she picked him up.

He wasn't sure if he should let her at first; didn't know if he could trust her. He knew he could wriggle free if he had to and he had his claws if she needed some persuasion. He'd go, he decided; see where she was going to take him. It had to be better than this place.

She carried him out of the building he had slept in and across the road into a small house. It was different from the one he was used to, full of the smell of people and of damp. As soon as they were inside it he squirmed free of the girl and dropped lithely to the floor. He wanted to look around. Find out what was here and how he could get out if he had to. The girl was one thing but he knew there would be other humans here. He could sense them; the scent of them invaded his nose and set him tingling.

Behind him she was talking urgently. She sounded upset but he couldn't tell why. Not just because he'd jumped down surely? He turned and looked quizzically up at her trying to understand what was causing this distress. Without warning she lunged forward and tried to pick him up again. He dodged her clumsy hands easily, jumping to one side and causing her to cry out with frustration. Keeping his eyes on her, wary now, he backed up slightly and lay on the floor, pressing himself low against it. The girl started talking again, pleading with him it seemed.

There was a noise from one of the other rooms. A banging and the deep, loud sound of a man's voice. Was that it? Did the girl not want the man to see him?

Marx heard heavy footsteps coming towards them. The girl reached for him, her eyes open wide and staring at him. She looked frightened. Marx felt the same way, felt a definite unease at the sound of the approaching man. Part of him wanted to run straight out of the house but he knew that if he did that he had nowhere to go. He looked at the girl, bending forward to pick him up and made his decision. He lifted his belly slightly, let her slide her hands under him and scoop him up. She lifted him awkwardly, her small arms struggling a little with his weight, and then pulled him tight against her.

Marx tensed as he heard the man getting closer, wondering what the child was going to do. Rather than run from the room she walked carefully across it to a large chair like the sort Walking and Sleeping used to sit together on when Sleeping was out of bed. The girl stepped up on to it and dropped him over the back. He lay down as soon as he hit the floor, understanding that she meant him to keep out of sight. The musty smell was overpowering there. It filled Marx's nostrils and made his head ache. The sound of the man's heavy footsteps increased and then stopped. His loud, gruff, harsh voice bounced off the bare walls as he spoke to the girl. Marx didn't like that voice. It sounded like danger to him, filled to the brim with anger that might spill out at any moment. There was a thud and the seat suddenly shifted backward, the stinking fabric pushed even closer to Marx's complaining nose. The cat tensed, ready to run, thinking the man had sensed him somehow. Smelled him or heard him or seen some sign of him. His tail twitched, the end of it tapping the back of the seat, and he willed it still. There was silence for a moment and Marx thought that one tap had given him away. The seat moved again. Marx stood, crouched low to the ground, every muscle he had prepared for flight. A voice filled the room, not the man, not the girl. Marx was confused at first and then he realised it had the hollow quality of the voices that came from Walking and Sleeping's screen. The man was watching something. Not looking for Marx, just relaxing.

The girl's face appeared briefly in front of him in the gap between the seat and the wall. She smiled at him reassuringly then put a little finger up against her lips. Marx had seen Walking and Sleeping do that in the past. He didn't know what it meant but he thought she was telling him to stay where he was. She certainly wasn't calling him to come out. He decided that was it and that he should trust her. Trust her and his ability to wake up in an instant. He closed his eyes and went to sleep.

It was the sound of her voice rather than a threat that roused him. He opened his eyes to see her face gazing down at him. She'd pulled the seat out a little and was crouched next to him talking to him earnestly. Marx decided he needed to name her. He toyed with the idea of Girl but decided that wasn't quite right. Little One. That would do. As for the man it had to be Loud.

He didn't know how long he'd been asleep for but he knew he was hungry. Little One tried to wriggle a hand under him to lift him up. He saved her the trouble, standing and craning up a little to nuzzle her face. As he did it he mewed at her twice, once to thank her for hiding him from Loud and once to tell her to get him some food. She scooted back and stood up; Marx trotted out of his hiding place after her. Loud was gone, the room was empty as it had been when he first entered it. The screen was off too and apart from Little One's musical voice everything was silent. She walked out of the room, waving at him to follow. Marx had a long satisfying stretch and then went after her. She'd obviously understood him because they walked through a small hallway and into a room that smelled of food. Marx remembered what had happened in the food room in Walking and Sleeping's house. Remembered the heat and the smell and the crackle. He sniffed the air deeply and while it didn't smell that good it didn't have the scent of danger either. He relaxed.

Little One pulled herself up onto a chair and opened a door there. She pulled out a metal thing, smaller than the ones Walking kept his food in. Was it food? He felt his stomach rumble as she pulled a ring on the top. A glorious oily, fishy smell hit his nose and his mouth filled with saliva. He jumped up, his front paws against the girl's legs, encouraging her to hurry up as she struggled to pull the lid fully off. That done she tipped the fish inside onto a dish and put it on the floor in front of him. She said something as she did it but he was beyond caring. The fish was good and went down quickly, salty and slippery and rich and nutritious. While he ate it Little One poured milk into a bowl. As soon as the fish was finished Marx started lapping at it, not finishing until his belly was satisfyingly full. He looked up at Little One and mewed. She was staring down at him with a look of happiness and pride so strong that Marx could almost feel the warmth of the emotions radiating out of her.

She nodded at him and then led him back out of the room and up some stairs. Marx followed happily, bounding after her with renewed energy. Little One took him to a room with a bed in it. Like the one that Sleeping slept in but smaller and with bright pictures of people and animals all over the walls. There were quite a few cats there, he noticed, although none quite as handsome as he was. He decided he could be happy here, for a while at least. As long as he kept out of Loud's way.

He curled up on the bed and watched Little One move about the room. She brought a small box out with a blanket in it and he decided that was where she wanted him to sleep. They would see how that went. There was another box with paper in it and he realised that this was for his toilet.

Little One pointed at them both in turn, talking with her light happy voice. He gazed at her from the bed and let her talk, then when she had finished he closed his eyes and went back to sleep.

When he woke up it was dark and the girl was asleep on the bed next to him, one small hand resting on his side. He wondered at first why he had woken up and then he heard the noise. A shout and then a bang from downstairs. He recognised the boom of Loud's voice and immediately tensed. There was another thud and a cry, not from Loud, from someone he hadn't heard before. A woman. There was silence for a while and then the low sound of people talking. Marx looked at Little One. The room was dark but he could make her out. She was still sleeping. Peaceful. Unalarmed by the noises that were making Marx think he should run from the room and from the house as quickly as he could.

He didn't know whether he should stay where he was or hide or flee. Then he heard a footstep on the stairs. His instincts made his decision for him. He leapt off the bed and then turned and ran under it, crawling as far to the back as he could. He circled once, checking the area around himself and then lay down and watched the room.

The footsteps were getting closer, climbing the stairs rapidly. Marx kept absolutely still, painfully aware that his twitching tail had nearly betrayed him before.

A blade of light cut through the darkness in the room as a door opened. A woman walked in, she looked unsteady on her feet to Marx, like she might fall over at any moment. She pushed the door closed behind her and walked towards the bed. It creaked a little as she sat on it. The wooden slats above Marx's head bowing slightly and then it settled again. He lay there and listened. At first there was only the sound of Little One and the woman breathing and then he heard the woman begin to cry. She was quiet about it at first but then the sobs got louder and louder. The bed rocked in time with them, making Marx feel like it was that which was crying not the woman. Marx had heard Walking cry like this sometimes, late at night when Sleeping was asleep and she was alone downstairs. He knew it wasn't good.

Little One must have been awoken by it because he heard her voice then, low and soothing, and the sobs quietened a little. The woman started speaking and then Little One spoke back and then the woman cried again. Then Little One did something that surprised him. He saw her tiny feet on the floor in front of him and then her face as she bent and looked under the bed for him. She saw him at once and spoke to him, her tone encouraging, friendly. He decided it was safe to come out.

As soon as he was out from under the bed Little One lifted him up and placed him next to the woman.

She looked at him surprised, her face shiny with tears even in the dim light of the room. Then her hands wrapped around him and she pulled him tight against her. Marx let her because he knew it was what Little One wanted. The three of them slept together in the small bed until morning.

When he woke up it was Little One that was crying. The woman was speaking to her seriously, pointing at him and shaking her head from side to side. Marx didn't know what it meant but he guessed it wasn't good. Little One put her arms around him and buried her face in his side. Her sobs vibrated through him and he felt the dampness of her tears through his fur.

The woman walked out and Little One just held him for a while then she got up too. Marx followed her downstairs. She didn't stop him which he took to mean Loud wasn't there. They ate together. Marx was given an egg and some milk.

When he had finished the woman picked him up. She took hold of the collar around his neck and inspected it. Then she said something to Little One who started crying again. The girl took him into the other room and cuddled him on a chair. Marx was beginning to feel uneasy. Was beginning to feel that the woman wanted him gone. Could he find his way back to Walking and Sleeping? He didn't think so, although it would be nice to see them again.

The woman came in to the room with a box and before he could get out of her way she had picked Marx up and put him in it. The lid closed quickly, closing him in to the small dark space. Marx struggled, scratching at the walls around him and the roof above his head but it did no good. He was trapped. He hissed loudly, angrily but from outside the darkness there was no response. Knowing there was nothing else he could do he lay down and slept.

He was in the box for a long time being carried he didn't know where. The motion was strangely soothing and he missed it when finally it stopped. The lid opened and the woman reached in to pull him out. They were outside. In a garden in front of a house. Marx looked around and realised that the garden was familiar, that he had looked at it many times. This was Walking and Sleeping's house. Something was wrong with it though. The windows he had gazed out of so many times were covered with boards and the walls around those boards were black. That smell was still in the air. The harsh smell that had hurt his nose and accompanied the heat.

The woman walked to the front door and knocked on it, Marx held tight against her with her other hand. The three of them stood there in silence, Little One looking sadly up at him. The door didn't move.

The woman muttered crossly and walked to the next house along the street. She repeated the knocking and this time a small wrinkled man opened the door. Marx recognised him. He was someone he had seen through the window.

The man shook his head when Little One's mother started speaking. He pointed at Marx and at the house and he waved his hands in the air. They talked like that for a while and then the woman nodded her head tiredly and turned back. She put Marx into the box and closed the lid.

When the box opened again Marx found he was back in Little One's room. He stayed there all day. Letting her stroke him and feed him, using the toilet area she had made for him, sleeping. Marx heard Loud elsewhere in the house at times, laughing his booming laugh and shouting and banging. Each time he heard him the cat felt a pull as his instincts told him to run. He sensed a similar tension in the girl too. A sadness. Then she would stroke or tickle him again and they would both be happier.

The woman came and looked in on them a few times, staring at Marx with a look of concern. He suspected that he didn't have long here, that the woman would try to put him out of the house at some point. There wasn't much he could do if she did though, so he decided to just enjoy his time with Little One. He couldn't remember ever being given as much attention as she gave him, Walking had always been too busy.

When night-time came Little One climbed into the bed and went to sleep. Marx curled up next to her and closed his eyes.

The same noises woke him as had the previous night. Loud's hard angry voice and the terrifying thudding that accompanied it. Little One woke up too. She swung her legs out of the bed and walked to the door. Marx didn't want her to go, didn't want her to leave the safety of the room. He mewed at her and she turned and looked at him silently, her eyes half closed with sleep. Then she turned back and opened the door. Marx ran after her.

The noises were louder when they got out of the room. Harsher. Little One walked to the top of the stairs and started down them. Marx could hear the woman crying again. He walked after the girl his tail lashing from side to side as he did. He wanted to keep close to her. If he couldn't stop her he could at least be with her.

When she pushed open the door to the front room the shouting stopped for a moment. Marx looked through the girl's legs to see the woman backed up against a wall and Loud standing in front of her. His fist was raised and the woman was clutching her stomach.

It was the first time he has seen the man. He looked like he sounded. Big and aggressive and threatening. His face was flushed with anger, beads of sweat popping on his brow and his eyes wide.

Marx watched the man's face change when he saw Little One. The rage was wiped-away for a moment and replaced with a look of sadness and surprise. Then Loud's eyes flicked down and locked onto Marx. The anger came back immediately. His jaw set firm and his eyes blazed.

Loud started shouting again; left the woman behind and walked towards Marx and the girl. Little One stepped forward and was pushed aside; she fell awkwardly to the floor and started crying. The woman shouted weakly and Loud turned back and roared at her. Marx backed away, terrified, not knowing whether he should run or fight. He knew he couldn't beat Loud but something was telling him to protect Little One. That this fight was worth it even if he didn't win. He stood his ground as Loud turned back to him. The room was still echoing from his shouts. Marx hissed at him, stating his intent. The man's giant hands reached down and the cat lashed out. His claws raked the skin on the back of one of them, tearing through it and drawing blood. Loud roared again. His other hand grabbed Marx by the neck and jerked him up. Marx's legs flailed as he tried to reach the man's flesh with his claws. He managed one more scratch before Loud hurled him across the room.

This was worse than falling, far worse. He had no control at all, was able to do nothing but thrash helplessly in the air as he flew through it. His back hit the wall and then his head snapped against it. He felt something snap inside his side, the pain sudden and intense and terrifying.

Marx fell to the floor stunned. He could hear Little One crying and the woman screaming and Loud shouting. The man's voice rose over everything else; obliterated his mate's and his child's. Marx turned his head and watched as Loud walked towards the woman and forced her back against the wall. Marx could see the bright blood on the back of his hand as he clenched his fist again and slammed it into the woman's stomach. She crumpled to the floor sobbing. Loud shouted one last time and then walked out of the room. The last thing Marx saw before his eyes closed was Little One running to the woman and putting her arms around her.

When he woke up everything was dark and his whole body hurt. He moved a leg and realised he was in the box again. He could feel it moving, rocking slightly as someone carried it. He shut his eyes and slept.

He awoke again to the sound of Little One's voice and the feeling of her hand stroking his head. He looked up and saw her leaning over the box, talking softly, comfortingly, to him. The woman appeared behind her and reached down to lift him out of the box. He mewed as her hands closed around his injured body. She murmured to him as she held him. He could tell she was doing it as delicately as she could but it still hurt.

As soon as he was out of the box Marx could see where he was. He recognised the room instantly but didn't understand why they were there. It was the main room of Walking and Sleeping's house but different from what he remembered. Dark from the shutters over the windows, lit just by a small lamp on the floor. It was filled with that harsh smell and the walls were blackened in places. Why had the woman brought them here? Maybe just because it was somewhere they could go that was away from Loud. Somewhere safe. Despite the smell and the feelings of fear it brought back Marx felt safer there than he had at Little One's house because he knew that Loud was far away.

There was a bowl of water and he drank thirstily from it before laying down on the floor as he had so many times before. Little One lay next to him with the woman next to her and the three of them slept.

He dreamt of Loud, of the sound and the heavy masculine smell of him. In the dream he could feel that strong hand gripping him but this time rather than throwing him Loud got his other hand on him too and twisted. Marx felt his spine twist and his guts wrench inside him. Then, mercifully he was woken up.

The voice that brought him out of the dream was a familiar one. It was Walking. She was talking to the woman and sounded at first surprised and then angry. When Marx stood up and walked painfully towards her though she gave a squeal of delight. She crouched and stroked him, talking with a concerned tone first to him and then to the woman when she saw that he was hurt. Marx watched her face the whole time and no matter what her voice sounded like her face looked the same. It looked tired and sad.

Once she had finished stroking him she sat cross legged on the floor and spoke to the woman. They spoke for a long time and during the conversation both of them cried. At one point they wrapped their arms around each other and hugged. Marx didn't pay too much attention though; Little One was awake too now and soothingly stroking his head and neck.

At last Walking stood. It seemed to Marx that some agreement had been reached between the two women but he didn't know what it was or what it meant for him. The woman also stood and called to Little One to go with her. Marx followed and together the four of them walked to the front door of the house. The two women were talking and the girl was busy looking at him and stroking the tip of his tail. Marx saw it first, the large shape through the blackened glass of the door. He meowed urgently, loudly, but rather than looking where they were supposed to, at the danger, the humans all looked at him.

The door slammed open and there was Loud. He stood there with the daylight streaming around him into the dark house. His thick body blotted out a portion of the light and his shadow fell across them all. He had something in his hand, a long, rounded, solid looking length of wood. He shouted as soon as he saw them, stepped into the house and reached out with his free hand to grab the woman by the wrist. She screamed and pulled back from him, struggling fiercely but unable to escape his strong grip. Walking shouted and stepped forward, her hands out in front of her to strike the man. He swung the wood and it hit one of her raised forearms with a crack. She fell to the floor clutching the arm which Marx saw was bent in a way it shouldn't be. Beside him Little One was screaming, the sound of fear and sorrow pouring out of her tiny mouth.

Loud shouted again, pulling the woman towards him. She looked back as he did, first at Little One and then at Marx. Something changed on her face. There was still fear there but there was suddenly a determination too. It came not when she looked at the girl but when she saw Marx's bloodied and swollen body. She turned back to the man and swung her leg at him, bringing her foot up hard between his legs. He gasped and let go of her hand. The wood he was holding fell to the floor and both his hands went to clutch his groin. He bent forward and Marx bounded forward and leapt up at him. His claws dug in on either side of Loud's face, holding him steady as his sharp teeth bit down into the man's cheek. The blood was hot and rich and reminded Marx of the daydreams he used to have about the birds in the garden. Loud let out a cry of pan and rage, one hand gripping Marx again and trying to pull him off. Marx dug his claws in deeper, the muscles in his legs straining against the force Loud was exerting. The hand squeezed him tighter, one of the fingers pushing against his broken rib, grinding the jagged ends of the bone against each other. He bit down even harder, his teeth meeting through Loud's flesh. He could hear the women shouting and Loud roaring but above them rose the light sound of Little One's voice. She was calling him, calling him back to her. He didn't know why but he trusted her. For the first time he trusted a human. He let go, retracting his claws and dropping from Loud's face, letting the chunk of flesh fall from his mouth. The moment he felt his feet hit the floor he heard a swishing sound and then a sharp crack as the woman brought the length of wood down on the back of Loud's head. Marx turned and ran back to Little One, getting out of the way just before the man crashed to the floor unconscious.

Lots of things happened after that. Blue lights and men and talking. Lots of talking. Marx let it all pass him by, playing with Little One and sleeping. Hoping that the pain in his side would go away and remembering how good Loud's hot blood had tasted.

When it was all over they stayed together, went to a new house where the four of them lived and healed. Marx and Walking and Little One and the woman. There was a bond between them now. A tie that came from standing side by side and fighting Loud.

On the third day there Marx realised two things. The first was that he never had given the woman a name. He decided to leave it just as it was. She would be called The Woman because that was what she was. Strong and fierce and proud and female. The second thing was that he didn't know where Sleeping was, he still hadn't seen her. Probably sleeping, he decided and went to find Little One.

A Cat Called Hope Returns

Now

Marx was running through the night, the cold wind blowing through his long fur and sending tingles down his whiskers. His heart was racing in his chest, beating so fast it felt like it was going to burst out of him and run on ahead. He had never run so fast or so far, not even when he had run from the fire that destroyed his home. This time though he wasn't running from danger he was running towards it. He had to, if he didn't the one human he cared about, the only person who meant anything to him, would be gone. The girl. Little One.

Before

Marx lived with the women and the girl for a while. Long enough for him to get used to it, this new way of being. Their names were stuck in his head and hadn't changed. The older woman was still Walking because that's what she did, constantly moving, doing, fussing. When he'd lived with her and Sleeping he'd thought that energy came from her need to care for the other woman. Now that Sleeping was gone the energy was still there and Marx realised it was just who she was.

Little One was as she had been since she'd found him cold and lost. She was kind and excited and sometimes Marx wished she'd leave him alone. Only sometimes though, most of the time he relished her attention.

Little One's mother, who Marx called simply The Woman, somehow managed to look after all of them without bustling like Walking did. She was always calm and sometimes a little sad. She made him feel safe.

So he lived with them, the three females, and enjoyed it. Then one day things changed. Marx found himself sitting at the window staring out of it at the grass and the birds. He remembered what that greenness tasted like and what it felt like under his paws and he realised that something out there was calling to him.

That was the start of it.

The next day Marx found himself there again. Staring again. Staring out. He couldn't decide if what had happened to him last time he went outside had been good or bad. He remembered being cold and wet and miserable but he remembered joy too. The thrill of running with no need to stop and of smelling things. The feel of the fresh chilled air streaming up his nose and through his body. He wanted it again.

Little One came and sat next to him and put her arm around him. Some days she dressed in drab clothes and left house early and was out all day but this wasn't one of those days. She spoke to him in her light voice, talking happily to him. He purred and nuzzled her putting his scent on her so other cats would know she was his. The girl squeezed him tight and he forgot all about outside for a while.

The next day Little One left early in her colourless clothes and Marx found himself drawn to the window again. The sun was shining out there and he could feel some of the warmth of it through the glass. He wanted to feel it properly though. The heat. Everything.

Outside a vehicle pulled up, white with flashes of colour along the side and blue glass bumps on the top of it. Two people climbed out of it; a man and a woman. Both were dressed in blue much darker than the glass or the sky. Marx watched as they walked towards the house. This was unusual, other humans didn't come here. He could see that they were talking to each other as they approached and that when they got to the door they stopped. Leaning forward so his face was touching the glass he could see the woman raise her hand and knock. Three sharp bangs that reached his ears as her fist hit the door.

Marx jumped down from the window sill and walked through to the hallway just as Walking opened the front door. He thought for a second about making a run for it, darting about past the two strangers and out into the world. He didn't because their presence made him feel uneasy, like he did before a storm. He wanted to watch them, to make sure they weren't bringing trouble to the house and the women. The blue woman spoke in a low voice. Walking nodded and stepped to one side letting them in. Marx could see her face as she did it. She looked afraid. Fear was something he hadn't seen on her face for a while and it made him frightened too.

The three humans sat and talked. Marx prowled around the edge of the room feeling restless, watching the three of them. The two visitors were trying to calm Walking with their monotonous talking and soft tones but he could tell they were failing. She was as full of nervous energy as he was, hands twitching in her lap, feet tapping on the ground like she wanted to be walking.

Eventually they left. Walking stood at the window and watched them go. Marx wound himself around her legs, purring at her, letting her know he was there. She reached down and stroked his head absent mindedly. When he looked up at her he saw that her eyes were shiny with tears.

When The Woman and Little One came home that evening Marx had almost forgotten about the visit. He had spent the afternoon sleeping and staring out of the window while Walking fussed around the house. As she always did when she arrived home, the girl ran to him and picked him clumsily up and hugged him. He relaxed and let her, watching as Walking went to The Woman and took her hand. The two of them walked into the kitchen together; through the glass door he could see them talking. The Woman turned away and her body started shaking making Marx feel like this was a private moment, one he shouldn't be witnessing. He wriggled out of Little One's arms and ran out of the room and up the stairs. She chased after him, giggling and calling his name.

Marx stopped when he reached the top and watched her awkwardly coming after him. She didn't have the grace that he did or even of adults like The Woman. He loved her like she was one of his own though. He realised that looking back at her, not in a conscious way but in a wave of emotion that hit him like the breeze through an open window. He looked at her and wondered if his eyes looked his father's had. Warm and full of pride and care.

Downstairs he could hear the two women talking. Walking sounded low and calm, The Woman distraught. Marx meowed at the girl, encouraging her to quicken her pace up the stairs. He doubted that she would but maybe at least she might focus on the sound of him rather than the pain of her mother.

She made it eventually, without looking back, and he ran from her into her bedroom, leaping up onto her bed and snuggling down. He knew she would join him and that she would quite happily spend an hour or two stroking him and cooing to him while the women downstairs sorted out their business.

Later on The Woman called up to let Little One know that her food was ready. The girl trotted down and Marx followed. The two women sounded calm but when they moved it was in a jerky way that reminded Marx of the quick, nervous motions of the birds he liked to watch through the window. There was no joy in the meal either, none of the laughter that normally filled the house like sunshine. Marx sat in silence and watched them. His heart felt like a stone, cold and hard in his chest, pulling him down.

The next day things appeared normal. Little One and The Woman got up and there was lots of rushing around and loud talking. All the busyness and noise made it hard for him to tell if there was still something wrong. They left the house with the girl in her drab clothes and Marx and Walking were left alone.

Marx sat and watched her for a clue as to what had happened the day before. For a while she just stood there with a look on her face that worried him. Was she sad or frightened? Marx wasn't sure but he could tell she was still disturbed. Then she launched into action as she so often did when the others were out of the house. She started walking busily around, moving things and making noises and funny smells. He wandered to where she was, wary of the thing in her hand which he knew sprayed a foul smelling cloud when she pressed the top of it.

She saw him and smiled, reaching down with her empty hand to scratch him behind the ear. He began to relax. This was all comfortingly normal, like so many other days had been since he'd moved to the house. Marx walked to his bowl and drank some water from it and then sat next to it. He watched Walking being busy and stopped worrying so much. There was a natural rhythm to things now that soothed him.

After a while he left Walking to her activity and walked to a window. He jumped softly up to the sill and sat there staring out at the warm summer day. That urge for freedom came back to him. He wanted to feel it, to explore it. Wanted the air in his lungs and the grass beneath his paws and the sun on his fur. He could hear Walking bustling about, tidying and cleaning. His tail waved back and forth as he sat there watching the green world outside and thinking. He wanted it so much. Like he wanted food in the morning when he caught the first scent of meat as the tin was opened. Now was the time, he decided. This was the day to run free. Just for a while and then he'd be back in the house before the girl got home.

He jumped down and walked to the kitchen where the woman was working. He knew if he sat there for long enough she would open a door and eventually she did.

Marx ran. He heard her gasp and the sound of the black bag she had been carrying hitting the floor. He felt her fingers brush the tip of his tail as he flew past but by then it was too late; he was out. He kept running, knowing she would chase after him and that if she caught him she'd scoop him up and no amount of struggling would get him out of her strong hands. He was in the garden at the back of the house, head twitching left and right to take it in. It was a space he'd looked at many times from the safety of the house, gazing on it with longing. Now he was out in it and it felt bigger, more terrifying and more wonderful. It was surrounded on all sides by a wooden fence which was as tall as any of the humans he knew. Too high for him to clear with a jump. Marx looked around and saw Walking emerging from the house. He ran from her, eager to enjoy as much freedom as he could. He would go back the house when he wanted to not when she dictated.

He chose a fence at random; he didn't know what was beyond any of them so just ran for the one that had caught his eye. His legs powered him across the grass, Walking was to one side of him, lunging at him, her hands grabbing but easily avoided. His muscles tingled as he ran; it felt good, so good. Just before he reached the fence he jumped, springing forward through the air. His paws met the rough wood, claws extended and dug into it. He scrambled up it, all four legs struggling as he climbed. The muscles started to burn and he thought for a moment that he wouldn't make it. He could see himself falling back down to the dirt, twisting his body in mid-air so he landed on his feet. He saw in his mind Walking picking him up and carrying him back to the house; heard her cooing at him and scolding him as she did it. He cared for the woman but at that moment the thought of her voice made him feel ill. As he climbed he heard her voice for real, shouting at him. She thinks she can stop me with it, he thought. Instead the feel of it hitting his ears gave him the strength to carry on.

His legs jerked like they had minds of their own and carried him to top of the fence. He perched there for a second and looked back at Walking. Her face was red and she shouted at him again. Should he go back? For a moment he thought he should. His tail lashed behind him as the indecision rose up inside him. It gave physical form to the battle within him between his animal nature and his addiction to the comfort the humans provided.

Behind him there was a great flapping of wings and he turned to see a cloud of birds rising up from a tree. They turned the sky dark, flocking together like a single living thing. Oh how he wanted them. Wanted so much to feel one fluttering beneath his paws as it tried to escape them. He looked back at the woman and mewed at her to let her know there were no hard feelings then he jumped away from her and down into the garden on the other side of the fence. His paws sunk slightly into the soil. It felt damp and cool and alive. A living thing itself just as he was.

He sprang forward onto the grass and ran across it. He could feel each of the thin green blades on the pads of his feet, caressing them in a way the artificial floors on the house never did. In front of him a worm wriggled across the lawn and he stopped to examine it. He slowly put a paw forward and touched it. He could feel the life pulsating through it. It was like the last time he'd been outside but better because this time he was here on his own terms.

There was a sound behind him and then he heard Walking's voice again, calling him. He turned and saw her standing there framed in a doorway. He realised that he had run not away from the house but around it. He'd left it through the back and was now in front of it. She lunged forward, her wrinkled hand brushing across the back of his neck but the old fingers were too slow to grab him. He flew forward, leaving the woman behind, his legs powering him over the grass. He would have liked to stop to enjoy it, maybe eat some as he had before. He knew if he did she would catch him or tempt him back inside somehow so he just kept going past the end of the grass and onto the dark hard ground beyond it. This felt good, the running. Not like last time when he'd been running from the fire. This time he was doing it because he wanted to.

There was a step down and he carried on, leaping off it. His legs stretched out in the air as he flew through it, the air ruffling his fur. He landing gracefully, knees bending to absorb the shock, and then was moving again. He heard the car before he saw it, the throb of the engine reaching his ears and raising him out of the thrill of the run. He turned and saw it approaching him. Big, black and threatening. Marx pushed himself harder, heart racing with the thrill of it, and dodged in front of the car easily. He hadn't felt so alive for months. There was a step ahead and he took it in his stride, carrying on along a short path and then around the side of another house. Up ahead he saw an alley, a tempting narrow gap running away from the street. He ran for it, not knowing where it went and not caring.

The walls on either side streaked past him as he shot through it but what he saw at the end made him slow. A constant stream of cars were passing the end of the alley. He thought about the one that he'd just dodged. That had been alone, these ones were flocking together. Could he avoid all of them? He looked behind him. Walking wasn't here, if she was chasing at all he knew she would still be some way behind him so he slowed to a walk. The noise grew as he approached the end of the alley until it filled his ears and made him dizzy. The wind from the passing vehicles ruffled the fur on his chest as he sat and watched them. The stench of them was as offensively alien as the cleaning sprays that Walking used around the house. It was a dirty sickening smell that he vaguely remembered from his last time outside. He wanted to get away from them but he wasn't ready to go back to the house yet. He would in time but he needed more freedom first and he could see that freedom across the road, a wonderful lush meadow full of high pale grass of a kind he had never seen before. Even over the dirty metallic odour of the cars he could smell the grass. Enticing and alive with possibility. What creatures lived in there?

Scampering and scuttling with their hot rich blood coursing through their little furry bodies.

He looked at the cars again, wondering if he could get past them. Daring himself to do it.

There seemed no end to them, a constant stream of noise and filth. And then he saw a gap, a space between two of them bigger than most. He tensed his body and waited until it was in front of him and then launched himself forward. His long sleek legs powered him forward and he passed with ease through the gap, the two cars safely distant from him on either side. His eyes focussed on the far side of the road, on the tall green grass there. What would it be like to run through it, those long fresh blades touching his sides, stroking him?

He didn't see the car coming from the other direction until it was on top of him. The shiny metal grill at the front suddenly looming over him. He stopped and flattened himself, surrounded by the roar and the wind as it passed over him. And then it was gone and the momentary absence of that roaring felt like a blessing.

He turned his head and saw another car approaching. The man inside saw him and his face was instantly painted with a mask of panicked horror. Marx stayed low, his belly pressed against the cold damp tarmac. That car passed over him too, the wind of it buffeting him, feeling like it would bowl him over and roll him down the street with the car.

He had to run again, had to get to that long lush grass and away from the noise and the metal and the acrid stink.

As soon as the car was gone he sprang forward, throwing himself towards the green. Another car was on top of him almost instantly. Loud and foul smelling and hot. It sounded angry, like an animal in a rage.

Beneath that roar Marx could hear the hum of the big black wheel on the road as he dodged in front of it. It was so close he could almost feel the pull of the rubber trying to suck him under it. He cleared it though, getting past just before it crushed him, his heart pounding in his chest like the wings of a bird beating the air. The wind from the wheel behind him lashed his tail, rocked it like a hand that had taken hold of it and was pulling it about.

He leapt off the road and into the grass turning in mid-air to look at the car that had nearly run him down. He hissed involuntarily as he did, not at the car, he understood enough to know that it was just a dumb thing that the humans used, but at the driver.

As his eyes focussed on the man his pounding heart beat even faster. It was Loud. Loud the man who had beaten The Woman, who had broken Walking's arm, who had nearly killed Marx.

Why was he here? Why was he back in their lives? Marx instantly felt the need to get back to the house. To be there for Little One when she got home. To protect her.

His momentum propelled him into the long thick grass but he didn't care about it now, all he wanted was to be home again. Could he warn Walking somehow? Would she understand?

He turned and looked back at the road through the green blades. He needed to get across it and down that alleyway. He looked to either side and then froze, his ears flattening and his back rising reflexively. Loud had stopped his car a short way along the road.

Marx watched from the grass as the car door opened and Loud climbed out. The man's head turned left and right, eyes searching the grass. He's looking for me, Marx realised and instantly pushed his body down. The grass felt cool and fresh beneath him and he regretted not having time to spend there.

Why had the man stopped the car? Because he knew Marx had seen him and was worried he would warn the women? Because he thought Marx could lead him to them? Was it just because he wanted revenge? Whatever the reason Marx knew he had to get back to the house. Get away from Loud and back to his family.

Laying flat as he was he couldn't see the man. He could hear his voice now though, deep and rumbling, as terrifying to him as the noise of the cars.

Should he run straight back across the road or try to evade Loud? If he went immediately to the house would Loud follow him? Would Marx be leading him right to the women and Little One?

He needed to be cunning, he realised, needed to be out of Loud's sight before he headed into the alleyway.

Marx slowly lifted his head, raising it up inch by inch so he could see through the tops of the grass as the blades thinned and spread higher up. He caught sight of the man thrashing at the grass with a stick, slowly walking towards him sweeping the grass to the left and the right as he advanced. The stick cut through the grass, sending the severed tips of it spinning through the air. He could hear the noise it made even over the traffic, the terrible swishing getting closer and closer. He knew he could just run away but doing that would only move him further from where he wanted to be. Instead he ran at the man, streaking through the grass, enjoying the feel of it parting before him and running along his flanks. The stick swept from left to right in front of him and he ran past it, aiming for the gap between Loud's parted legs. The return stroke slashed just behind the tip of his tail and he felt the wind of its passing.

Loud saw him and roared, turning and bring the stick straight down at him. It parted the grass above his head and swept down towards him. He could feel the air moving before it and then it struck, cracking down on the top of his skull with a force that sent shockwaves through his entire body. He kept running but staggered to the side, his body temporarily out of his control, his vision blurred from the blow. The top of his head throbbed and he could feel something warm trickling over his skin, through the strands of his fur. It ran down his nose and his tongue flicked up to catch it, the sweet rich taste of blood.

The shock of it was a reminder that he was just as fragile as everything else, that no matter how strong he felt running in the grass he could bleed like every other creature. And that meant he had to draw on every reserve of strength he had to escape the man who was stalking him.

He ran on as fast as he can, hearing another roar from Loud and looking back to see the man chasing after him. His head cleared as the air streamed through his lungs again. The clarity returned to his vision. Loud was closing on him, he could hear the pounding of his feet on the dirt getting nearer and nearer.

The road streaked past by his left flank as he ran, still busy with the rumble of traffic. He realised suddenly that it could be his salvation; that it might act as a wall to prevent Loud from following him. Loud was bigger and more powerful but that was something that Marx could use to his advantage.

He glanced at the road again. He was starting to understand the flow of it, the rhythm. The cars on one side went in one direction, the ones on the other went the opposite way. The cars on his side of the road were coming towards him, noisy and smelly and threatening.

One passed him and there was a gap, a space he could have run through to the middle of the road. He didn't dart out though, he waited, kept running through the grass with the cars road to his side. Loud was behind him, getting closer with every step, his long strides eating up the distance between them.

Another car came towards Marx and he could see more coming along behind it. He waited until it was close, so close. And then he ran into the road.

He made it into the path of the car and then froze, ducking down like he had on his way over the road. The car passed over him, the wind from it shaking him, almost lifting him up and bowling him over. He squashed himself down as flat as he could and then ran again as soon as the car had gone. The one behind was almost on him as he ran, bearing down on him like a great snarling beast, but he made it out of its path before those turning wheels caught him and pulled him under. He stopped in the centre of the road, the white line beneath his paws. Behind him he could hear the roar of the traffic and beyond that a yell of frustration from Loud.

Cars were coming at him from both sides now, two constant streams. He threw himself forward, flattened himself again and then ran the rest of the way to safety of the pavement. He looked back across the road when he got there and saw the furious Loud still stranded on the other side.

Marx didn't wait, he ran back along the pavement to the alleyway, the cars hiding him, when he reached it he looked back again and could see only the traffic.

The walls of the alley streaked past him and then he was back on the street where the women lived. He saw Walking and ran to her, letting her scoop him up into her arms. She cooed over him, touched his head gently, examining the wound there.

He stared up at her, trying to think of a way to tell her what had happened but failing to get anything more than sympathetic muttering from her.

She carried him back to the house and put him down on the floor in the hallway. He ran through to the other room, jumped up onto the windowsill and stared out at the world, watching for Loud.

He didn't hear her behind him until it was too late. Her strong hands lifted him and before he could escape she had placed him in the cage she had carried into the room and closed the door, fastening it shut. He was trapped. He meowed at her furiously, telling her to stop, that she mustn't stop him watching for Loud, but all she did was stare in at him and talk in that soft calming voice of hers. Then she stood, lifted the cage with him in it and carried him out of the house. She's taking me to the animal place, he thought, the place with the dogs and the other cats where they poke me and prod me. It's because of my head, he realised, because of what Loud did to it.

He looked all around him as she walked him to the car, turning around and around in the cage looking for signs of Loud. It was just as she opened the door and swung that cage onto the seat that he saw him driving slowly along the street towards the house. Surely she'll see him, he thought, she must do. She'll see him and do something. But she didn't. Walking just walked back around the car to the other side and climbed in next to him. He threw himself at the door of the cage, flinging his body against it to try and force it open but the door stayed firmly shut. He heard the engine start and meowed again, the longest, loudest caterwaul he could summon up. Walking tutted at him and started driving.

The car stopped just a few minutes later and she climbed out of the car and walked around it again. She lifted the cage out and carried him into the building she had parked outside. Marx was tensed and ready, knowing that he had to be ready to run as soon as the cage was opened. He could smell other animals around him, the strong scent of dog and cat and rodent. There was fear there and pain. The stench of urine and distress assailed his nostrils and made him long for the clean smell of the grass. His hackles rose as he heard a dog barking but he knew he couldn't let it distract him. He was lifted onto a table and a man in white peered into the cage. He said something to Walking and then reached forward to open the door.

Every muscle in Marx's body was prepared. His heart was racing, pumping the blood to every part of him ready to run. In the distance the dog barked again and then let out a howl of pain. Marx could see the man's fingers as they moved towards him. He watched them manipulate the catch that kept him imprisoned. He could see only the man and the wall behind him, could sense Walking off to one side but had no knowledge of what else was out there. Was there a route for him to escape through or was he would he trapped in the room as soon as he escaped the cage? Whatever the case he knew he had to try. For Little One.

The door of the cage swung open and the man's hands reached in to him. Marx threw himself forward, back legs kicking off the back of the cage and propelling him out onto the cold metal. He skidded across the table, the force of his movement pushing the cage back until it toppled off the other side of it and crashed to the floor. The man tried to grab him but Marx was too fast. Walking shouted, a mix of concern and annoyance in her voice. The door of the room was visible now, closed with no hint of a gap that he could squeeze through. Marx looked around himself, his head and tail swishing from side to side at either end of his lean body as he looked for a way out. And then he saw it, on the other side of the room from the door a small window set high in the wall was open slightly to let in a breeze. He jumped from the table just as the man tried to grab him again, flying gracefully through the air and landing on a metal counter that ran along the wall. His legs carried him over it, paws slipping on the shiny surface but still finding enough traction to carry him forward. A tall yellow bin stood on the countertop near the window and Marx leaped up onto it, feeling it tilt under his weight as he landed on it. He jumped again immediately and heard it fall over behind him as he did. His front paws landed on the sill of the open window and he dug his claws into it hanging on as his back legs scrambled frantically at the wall beneath it. The surface was slick, offering none of the rough purchase that the garden fence had. He felt the weight of his body dragging him down and thought for a minute that he would fall. Then slowly he realised that the strain on his front legs was lessening, that the claws of his back paws were starting to grip the wall and propel him up. He heard a shout behind him and struggled even harder lifting himself up until all four of his paws were on the narrow sill. Marx glanced back at the room quickly and saw the man lunging for him, trying to grab him and pull him back down. He thrust his head at the narrow gap of the open window, thrusting it out into the fresh air outside. The wood scraped the wound on his head and he mewed with pain but kept going, wriggling his body through the gap and then half jumping, half falling to the ground below. His front paws hit the concrete hard, legs flexing to absorb the impact. He could see Walking's car and ran to it and then past it, following the path he knew she must have taken and heading out onto the road. He stopped there, looking both ways, trying to decide which way home was. He hadn't been able to see out of the car as Walking drove him there but he had felt each turn. He reversed them in his mind, if he could track back at least some of the way he might have a hope of getting to Little One. The last turn had been to his weaker side, the one on which Loud had broken one of his ribs all those months ago. He turned the opposite way and ran, dodging the people on the street, eyes pointed ahead as he pushed himself to move as quickly as he could.

The next turn needed to be to his stronger side he thought, then weaker, then stronger again. He had no idea how far Walking had driven on each stretch but he knew how long they had taken. He tried to match his pace to the traffic on the road, running with it for the length of time he thought she had driven.

He ran and ran, desperately hoping to see something he recognised but knowing with each step that it was less and less likely. Loud was there. Waiting. As soon the Woman and Little One arrived home he would attack. Marx didn't know what the man would do but he knew he had violence in his heart, that he was incapable of tenderness. He knew that whatever Loud did would be bad.

He ran on, knowing there was nothing else he could do, that the only alternative was to stop. And then suddenly, miraculously, he knew where he was.

On the road with the grass by the side of it, the road where he had escaped Loud. He saw the alleyway up ahead and headed for it. His heart was beating hard inside him, not from exertion now but from fear. He had to stop Loud but he had no idea how he would do it.

He flew through the alleyway, coming out onto the road in time to see Loud's car starting to drive away. Little One was in the back of it, her hands pressed against the glass of the window, her face wet with tears. Marx saw The Woman laying on the floor, blood running from her nose and a gash in her forehead and pooling beneath her.

He looked away from her back at the car, the girl had seen him and was banging on the glass as Loud drove off. Marx ran at the car, his legs powering beneath him. At first he closed the distance but then gradually, terribly, the car started to pull away again. The more he ran the further away it got until he knew there was no way he could catch it. That he had no hope. He stopped and sank exhausted to the ground, his chest heaving, his head resting on his paws. Up ahead he saw the car drive on and then turn and pass out of his vision. It was gone, he had failed. It would be out on the main road by now.

It hit him with a force that shook him almost as much as Loud's blow had. The road. The road at the end of the alleyway.

He was on his feet in an instant, turning and running back the way he had come. The Woman was still there, raising herself onto one elbow now, her eyes open and full of fear. Marx ignored her, turning into the alley and charging down it. He reached the end of it and looked both ways and there, there it was, Loud's car driving toward him. He ran. Not towards it but in the same direction, knowing that it would reach him soon, reach him and pass him. He had one hope, one hope only and it rested with Little One. If she saw him, if she understood, then he might be able to save her. He looked over his shoulder and saw the car nearing him. Loud's red face behind the wheel, his dark eyes watching the road. Marx saw Little One beyond the man, her terrified face pulling at his heart. In that instant he could tell that she has seen him. He just hoped she understood.

He ran on, as fast as he could, the car close behind him now, almost drawing level with him. He heard her voice over the sound of the engine and knew that she had done what he needed her too. As the car came up by the side of him he saw her face through the window. The window she had lowered so that she could call to him.

Marx jumped.

Every leap, every pounce, every jump he had ever made was in preparation for this one. He knew if he didn't make it the wheels of car would crush him and Little One would be lost. Every part of it had to be perfect but it was not something to think about.

His brain shut down and his instincts took over. Every ounce of energy he had went to his legs.

The cat sailed through the air, the hard metal of the car to his side, the smell of it filling his nose. He could hear Little One's voice and see her mouth moving as he flew towards her and the open window.

The edge of the door frame caught his rear flank as he passed through it, spinning him in the air, twisting him around and sending a bolt of pain through his whole body. He landed in Little One's lap and stared up at her, his heart full of love and his body shaking with relief. He had done it.

From the front seat Loud roared with anger, turning and grabbing Marx by the neck with one big hand. The cat lashed out at him as Loud pulled him into the front of the car, claws scratching at that grasping hand, digging into the flesh on the back of them and tearing it open.

Loud roared again and swung Marx through the air, slamming his back into the window. His other hand was still on the steering wheel and the cat clawed at with his back legs as Loud squeezed his throat shut and banged him again and again against the glass.

He could feel his body shutting down as Loud's iron grip cut off his supply of air. His lungs began to ache and his vision darkened at the edges. Loud's face filled the narrowing circle of his view. It was ugly with rage and hatred, the eyes gleaming with a ferocious insanity. And then the eyes were gone, vanished suddenly and Marx's oxygen starved brain couldn't comprehend why. The pressure on his throat vanished and he fell into the man's lap. Looking up he saw that the place where Loud's eyes had been was now a pink blur of flesh, as if the man's skin had magically grown over them. As his senses returned he realised what he was seeing, Little One's hands reaching from the back of the car and covering her father's eyes.

Loud raised his torn and bloody hand and batted the girl's fingers away but it was too late. Marx was thrown into the air as the front wheels of the car hit the kerb and bounced up it. There was a tremendous crash and the whole car came to a shuddering halt as it smashed into a wall. The last thing Marx saw was Loud flying at the windscreen and then he too slammed into it and fell into unconsciousness.

When he woke up the man in the white coat was looming over him. Marx meowed softly and looked around the room, realising he was back in the place he had run from earlier. For a second he worried that he had imagined the car and the fight with Loud. Then he felt the ache in his throat and the throbbing in his back from where Loud had slammed him against the glass and he knew that it had really happened. Little One, he thought, he had saved her and she had saved him. Then the sharpness of a needle stabbed into him and he was asleep again.

Two days later he was home. He sat by the window looking out. He did not know where Loud was, had no idea if the man had lived or died but he would watch for him.

Behind him in the room Walking bustled around, fetching food and drinks for Little One and The Woman, caring for them as they recovered from their injuries. She is doing what she was designed to, he thought. Nurturing.

As he sat there looking out he realised that he too had a purpose. I will do what I was brought into their lives to do, he told himself. I will protect them. Always.

A Cat Called Hope – The Final Chapter

Time passed.

Marx was happy and so were the women; the older one, Walking, and the younger whom Marx called simply The Woman. And as for the girl, Little One, well she was happy too, and growing bigger by the day. They lived together in their little house and Marx did cat things and the women and the girl did human things and sometimes they did things together. When Little One was there he would let her play with him and when she wasn't he would sit by the window and watch the world outside.

Of course, it didn't last for ever and Marx had never thought that it would. He knew that as happy as they might be in any individual moment, Loud was still out there. Loud, the man who had beaten The Woman and cracked Marx's bones. Loud, the man who had terrorised his own offspring, Little One, and tried to take her away from the women. Marx had beaten him twice before and he would do it again if he had to. He would do it gladly.

Little One and The Woman mostly went out during the day and Walking fussed around the place. Sometimes she went out too, and on the day that Loud came back that was what she had done. Marx was alone in the house, sitting by the window as he did. Sitting and watching.

Marx didn't really understand the noisy, dirty boxes that the humans used to move from one place to another but he had come to recognise the ones that stopped outside the house. He knew the one that The Woman used and the one that belonged to the people who lived next door. He knew the large white one that came with bags and bags of food that Walking then spent hours putting into the kitchen cupboards; and he knew the red one that occasionally came with brown packages that made The Woman grin excitedly.

The vehicle outside was none of those.

Marx's eyes narrowed as he watched it pull up on the driveway outside the house and stop. He could just hear the low angry rumble that it made through the cold glass in front of him. The house was warm but he could feel the frigid winter air outside, had felt it when the Woman opened the front door that morning, an icy tentacle that had crept into the house and penetrated his fur. He could see the cold too, in the damp grey clouds that blotted out the blue of the sky and the wind that shook the branches and yellowing leaves of the trees.

The noise of the car stopped suddenly. Marx kept his eyes on it, the dull autumn light reflected off the windscreen and he could see only the dark silhouettes of the two humans inside it. The two doors opened as one, giving the vehicle the look of a beetle opening its shell to reveal its wings. The car didn't take off though, it just ejected its cargo, one man stepping out of each side, unfolding themselves and standing tall.

Marx's tail flicked behind him as recognised one of the men. Even from this distance he knew Loud from his arrogant gait. The man's body was filled with a power and aggression that raised the cat's hackles. Marx remembered the physical pain that Loud had inflicted on him and the nightmare of abuse that the man had put his wife and daughter through. The fact that he was here filled Marx with disquiet and tension. The cat had sworn to himself that he would fight Loud to protect the women and Little One, but he knew it would not be an easy battle.

Marx prowled up and down the window ledge, the cold glass by first one side of him then the other. His eyes stayed fixed on the two men the whole time. He could see the clouds of their breath as they spoke to each other but he couldn't hear them and even if he had he knew he wouldn't have been able to understand them. That frustrated him sometimes, he knew that humans packed a lot of meaning into the noises they made and he wished he could decipher them properly. He could usually catch some sense of what people meant to do, though, and he could tell that Loud and his companion had only bad intentions.

He watched them as they talked, preparing himself for the moment when they came closer, when they tried to get into the house. He knew that the front door was the most likely entry point and that he should run to the hallway to confront them; but he also knew that if he was there he wouldn't be able to see them. He would stay where he was for now. Stay and watch.

Loud looked different, older and more tired. His face was scarred and Marx remembered the sight of him after the crash, surrounded by broken glass and blood.

The other man lacked the cloud of raw violence that surrounded Loud, he was smaller, softer. His features had a symmetry and refinement to them which Loud's lacked but there was still an edge of unpleasantness to him, something that made the muscles in Marx's jaw ache. Maybe it was just the fact that he was with Loud but even from this distance the cat could sense something else about him. It was like his face was a mask, not really attached to his body or his soul. A layer of fleshy deceit that covered the raw truth of his skull.

Loud was gesturing now, pointing at the house. He stopped as his eyes met the cat's, and smiled a broken smile that suddenly seemed to fill Marx's vision. I will hurt you, those teeth said, any chance I get. The other man said something and Loud spat on the ground before he replied. Now, Marx remembered the taste of the man's blood rather than his own and wanted to taste it again. The other man laughed and again Marx saw the coldness inside him seeping through the mask of humanity he wore. Liar, he thought, you are The Liar.

Marx paced and waited, paced and waited; but when the men moved they got back into the car rather than walking towards the house. He stopped mid-step and watched the vehicle back away into the cloud of its own exhaust. The dirty smoke billowed around it until he couldn't see the two men through the retreating glass any longer and then the car span and was gone.

Why had they come and then left? What did they want? Whatever it was he knew it could be nothing good. He needed to be on his guard more than ever. He needed to protect his family.

When Walking came back later Marx meowed at her and danced around her legs but she simply scolded him and filled his food bowl with biscuits. He returned to the window and stared out of it at the empty road.

When The Woman and Little One walked in he tried the same with them. The girl laughed delightedly at his antics. Her mother bent down and scratched his head absentmindedly and then walked through to the kitchen and started speaking to Walking. Marx gave up.

While the humans went about their business he sat at the window and watched. There was no sign of Loud or the other man and he wondered again why they had come. There was no point in trying to understand humans, he decided, they did what they did with no rhyme or reason to it.

When Little One went upstairs to sleep that evening Marx followed her. He always slept on her bed but not usually for the whole night. He would get up to eat or drink or use his litter tray. He would prowl his kingdom enjoying the quiet and the darkness. On this night he did none of those things, he stayed curled up at the foot of her bed from the moment she fell asleep until she awoke in the morning.

She said his name as soon as she saw him and sat up to stroke him. Her small hands were warm on his back, her gestures clumsy but full of care. He looked at her and purred. He wouldn't let anything happen to her.

The days passed and nothing happened. Loud and The Liar didn't come back and Marx began to wonder if he had imagined seeing them. Had he dozed on the windowsill that day as he often did? Usually his dreams were of running outside. Of chasing and hunting. Occasionally of playing with Little One. Never of Loud. So, no, he did not think the man's appearance was anything other than reality, even if he couldn't explain the reason for it.

The women and the girl went about their lives as they always did and those days became weeks. Autumn turned to winter and the blast of air when the front door opened became even chillier. The humans put on more and more clothes when they went outside, wrapping themselves up until they were almost unrecognisable, even the way they moved altered by the layers of clothing they wore. Marx watched them as he licked his luxuriant fur and decided he couldn't blame them for wanting to cover their pale unclothed nakedness. A change came over The Woman during those weeks and, much like Loud's momentary reappearance, Marx couldn't explain it. She seemed more at ease with herself, happier. She would sit with Walking staring at the bright, noisy screen that they used for entertainment but Marx could tell her eyes weren't really on it. She was seeing something else, something that wasn't there at all. Whatever it was it made her happy and that pleased the cat, for a while at least.

And then one evening something happened and Marx understood everything. When he did he almost wished he hadn't.

It was dark and Little One was in bed. The Woman and Walking were acting strangely. The younger of the pair was dressed in an outfit Marx had never seen before, one she kept smoothing down with her hands and fussing over. Her face was painted with bright colours that accentuated her pleasing features and her hair was lifted up onto the top of her head somehow rather than hanging limply like it usually did. She looks proud he thought, like a cat with its tail held high. Walking kept buzzing around her like a cheerful fly, smiling and talking and touching The Woman's bare arms tenderly, her wrinkled hands in contrast to her friend's smooth unblemished flesh.

The doorbell rang and Marx's ears pricked up. He knew the sound well but he associated it with daylight not the darkness that now surrounded the house. He rose from his resting position by the warm radiator in the living room and trotted to the hallway, stopping and staring at the door suspiciously. The Woman hurried past him surrounded by a cloud of floral scent that prickled at his nostrils; she reached the door and stood still for a moment, taking a deep breath before reaching forward one hand. Marx noticed that the ends of her fingers were painted red like blood.

The door opened at her touch and let in a cold draught. The fresh air cleared the almost overwhelming stink from his nostrils and he welcomed that. Then he saw the figure on the other side of the door and forgot about the smell altogether. It was The Liar.

His dark eyes twinkled from the light flooding out of the house as he stood there on the doorstep smiling. Marx felt his back arch involuntarily and his hackles rise. He opened his mouth and hissed, his ears laying flat on his head and his claws emerging. He looked past the man to see if Loud was there too and saw that The Liar was alone.
Why was he here? Why was he smiling at The Woman and why was she smiling back. He said something and she giggled, sounding for a moment like Little One when she was playing one of her games. Marx hissed again and then lay his body flat

on the floor, creeping slowly towards the door, meaning to get near the man and then leap at him. The Liar seemed oblivious to him, as did The Woman. Their eyes were only on each other as they talked and smiled and laughed.

Walking had been watching him though, had seen his reaction and suddenly her old hands were sliding under his stomach and lifting him up into her arms. She held him tightly and scolded him softly, carrying him back into the living room and dropping him onto the floor. He made to run to the hallway again but she was too quick for him and pushed the door shut before he reached it.

She doesn't know, he realised, neither of them do, only I saw Loud and The Liar together. He turned and meowed at her, trying to make her understand, but she just shook her head and tutted at him.

Marx heard The Woman call something from the hallway and Walking replied and then came the sound of the front door closing. Walking opened the door from the living room then and Marx darted out. The Woman was gone. He has taken her, he thought, tricked her somehow into going with him and taken her to Loud. He threw himself at the door and clawed at the wood and at the matt in front of it, trying make a way out even though he knew it was futile. Walking spoke to him sternly, picking him up and making to carry him back to the living room. Marx twisted his body, wriggling free of her old hands and running up the stairs as fast as he could. He headed for Little One's room, squeezing through the gap between the door and the frame and padding softly in. His eyes adjusted and he saw the shape of her in the bed, the covers over her rising and falling almost imperceptibly as she slept. He walked to the foot of her bed and jumped lightly onto it, walking in circle and then laying himself down. He pointed his sharp nose at the door and rested his chin on his paws. Watching.

He dozed like that, waking every so often to watch the door and listen to the sounds of the house.

He didn't know how long he had been there when the sound of the front door opening woke him. He leapt from the bed, giving Little One a quick glance as he ran to the door and slipped back out through it. She still slept as if nothing had happened.

Marx didn't know what he would see when he reached the top of the stairs. Would Loud be at the doorway, stepping into the house? The Liar at his side grinning his fake smile.

He watched the door open and The Woman walked in, alone. She was smiling.

Marx ran down the stairs to her, rubbed himself against her legs and meowed a quiet welcome. He realised he hadn't expected to see her again.

She walked through to the living room and he followed, watching her as she sat and started talking eagerly to Walking. He regarded them both and felt his heart quicken with fresh fear. He didn't know what had happened that night but he was sure it wasn't good.

The women paid him no attention, too wrapped up in their conversation, so at last Marx turned and ran from the room, heading back up the stairs to the warmth of Little One's bed where he had both comfort and purpose.

Three or four nights later The Liar came again. The doorbell rang after dark and Marx knew who he would see when The Woman opened the door. This time rather than going out she invited the man in, and as he walked past Marx he bent to stroke the cat's head. Marx hissed and swiped a paw at the outstretched hand, claws extended, wanting to hurt the man, to warn him off. The Liar jerked his hand back, pulling it out of the way and whistling softly. He said something to The Woman and laughed. She turned and frowned at Marx then bent and picked him up, carrying him through to the kitchen and shutting him in there. He meowed loudly at her as she did it, narrowing his eyes and flattening his ears to show her there was danger but he could tell even as he did it that she didn't understand.

He paced in there, walking around and around the small white space. From the dining room next door he could hear the two of them talking and laughing. Don't trust him, he thought, that pink flesh is a lie, underneath it is a monster.

Walking came in at one point to fetch herself a drink. She stroked him and spoke soothingly and then left. He heard her walking up the stairs and realised that even she wasn't watching The Woman.

After a while The Woman came in carrying their plates, she placed them on the side and ignored Marx's cries. When she left the room he sank to the floor in despair. They didn't understand him, he couldn't make them see what The Liar really was.

The voices from the other room were quieter now, dropping in volume and frequency until they stopped altogether. The door opened slightly and he saw The Woman peering in at him then she turned and walked away. He ran after her, pawing at the door to open it enough so that he could get out. He reached the stairs in time to see her and The Liar walking up them. They walked into her bedroom and the door shut behind them.

Marx ran to Little One's room and jumped back onto the bed. He lay there in the darkness listening to the unfamiliar sounds coming from The Woman's room.

Marx rose when it was light, jumping down from Little One's bed and walking out into the hallway. The door to the Woman's room was still shut but he could hear the low murmurings of speech from the other side of it. He sat there, watching and then it opened and he saw the Liar's face. The man was naked except for some underwear, his legs and chest bare.

He was well muscled, not powerful like Loud was but there was still the suggestion of strength in his frame. His body is as deceitful as his face, Marx thought as he watched the man step out of the room, it looks normal, normal enough that The Woman trusts him, but beneath it his heart is full of corruption. She must have trusted Loud once too, he thought, somehow they fool her.

The Liar hadn't noticed him and the women were nowhere to be seen, The Woman must still be warm in her bed, Walking in hers. I need to let him know, the cat thought, he needs to know that I know what he really is and that he is not welcome here. His reaction to the man before had been instinctive but now it was calculated. I need to hurt him.

Marx pushed his body low against the floor and tucked himself against the wall. The Liar walked right past him, his sleepy eyes not seeing the cat in the half light of the early morning. He walked towards the bathroom and as he passed Marx turned and tensed his body. When the man was a foot away he leapt at him, his sinewy frame uncurling like a spring, front legs outstretched. He hit the man's thigh as he had hoped to and wrapped his front paws around the thick, muscular leg, releasing his claws from their tiny sheaths and digging them into the pale flesh. The claws on his rear legs came out too, scratching at the man's calf, as Marx's mouth opened and his pointed teeth bit down. He captured a flap of skin between them and felt a wave of primal pleasure as his teeth punctured it and he tasted blood.

The Liar yelled in fury and swung a heavy fist down at the cat's head. It collided and Marx had to blink his eyes to straighten his vision. He clung on though, claws scratching and his mouth biting again and again as The Liar howled and beat him. The man brought his other hand around, grabbing Marx by the throat and squeezing until the cat felt the bones in his neck grind against each other and saw clouds of darkness start to invade the edges of his sight. Then the fist slammed into him again and he fell to the carpet, dazed.

The Woman was there by then, she lifted him and held him close. He could feel her eyes on him as she carried him down the stairs. He looked into them and saw concern and confusion. And anger, he realised, she is angry with me. She dropped him on the hard floor of the kitchen and shut the door without a word.

Marx curled up on the floor and waited. He heard motion and talking in the hallway. The Liar's voice and The Woman's and then the front door opening and closing. He dozed for a while and then heard Little One. The Woman came in and prepared breakfast for the girl as she did every morning. As she left the room she looked at him and frowned.

Later, Walking came to him and carried him through to the living room. She sat with him on her lap and examined him, stroking him and talking to him. He didn't know what she was saying but he could tell she was worried. They must know I would never hurt them, he thought. Why don't they see what I see in him?

The Woman and Little One were both gone for the day so he spent his time watching at the window and listening to Walking bustle around the house. In the afternoon she left as she always did and he knew she would return with Little One before long. He looked forward to seeing the girl.

When the door opened he ran to them and nuzzled Little One's legs, making her giggle. She reached down to stroke him and he craned his neck up and rubbed his face against her hands, getting his scent on her. If The Liar came back he wanted him to know that they were under his protection, all of them.

Walking shooed him back and spoke to Little One who sat on the long, low seat by the door and started to take her shoes off. Marx nuzzled her legs and hands again and again and she stroked him behind the ear.

The ring of the doorbell came a minute later, while Walking was still struggling out of her heavy coat. She turned back to the door and opened it. Marx was still delighting in Little One's attention and he didn't look at the door until it was fully open and he heard Walking gasp.

The Liar was there, shouting at Walking, stepping up into the house and pushing her backwards. She shouted a warning at Little One and the girl froze for a second as Walking stumbled backwards and then she spun and ran up the stairs, one shoe off and one on. Marx watched as the old woman collided with the wall and sighed as the breath went out of her small frame. She righted herself quickly and stepped towards The Liar, blocking his way to the stairs. Marx danced between her legs as she moved, anticipating her direction and keeping out of her way. He knew he needed to help somehow but The Liar had easily defeated him last time.

The man pushed Walking again and she staggered back against the stairs and sat down heavily on them. He took a step forward, shouting and raising the same heavy fist that he had beaten Marx with. The cat knew he had to act. He jumped up onto the seat then jumped again, throwing himself at the wall and then pushing off it and going higher. He stretched his paws out as he had before but this time it was the Liar's head that he wrapped them around. The claws on his right paw caught one of the man's ears and dug into the sinewy tissue, the other paw landed on the back of The Liar's neck and Marx forced them into the flesh there. His back legs scrambled against the man's upper arm and chest, scratching through clothing and skin. Marx bit down on a fleshy cheek and relished the yell of anger and pain. The Liar grabbed at him and tried to pull him off but Marx held fast. He suddenly felt the man move violently and braced himself for an impact. Through one eye he was that Walking was on her feet again and that she had shoved The Liar backwards. Marx felt himself moving as the man clumsily tried to regain his footing, then the world tilted and Marx realised he was falling. He jumped free, flying through air and landing softly on cold damp grass as The Liar tripped over the doorstep and fell with a crash onto the concrete path. Marx looked with satisfaction at the damaged face, blood running freely from the cheek and ear. He saw something else, a small, dark square that had fallen from the man's pocket and lay to one side of him in the flower bed.

Walking was shouting and Marx turned to look at her standing tall and strong in the doorway, her face flushed and her eyes on fire. The man grunted and then scrambled to his feet and ran off down the path.

They sat in the living room later, the four of them, the women and girl fussing over Marx. He purred and let them stroke him, nuzzling The Woman to let her know he had forgiven her for punishing him that morning.

The doorbell rang and Marx was instantly alert but The Woman rose swiftly and without concern and walked out of the room to answer it. He ran after her and saw her open the door to two men in blue who entered the house and sat with the humans talking to them and scratching away at the flat white pads they had brought with them.

When they left, Little One went upstairs and the two women talked for a while and drank a dark red drink which seemed to relax them. Marx stayed by the window, sitting behind the curtains and looking out into the darkness.

He saw the shapes of the men lurch out of the gloom. Two of them, Loud and The Liar.

He turned frantically and slipped through the gap in the curtains, jumping onto the chair beside The Woman and meowing as loudly as he could. She looked at him with raised eyebrows then stood as he ran back to the window. She took a step forward and then stopped and he was worried she was going to sit again, instead she quickly paced across the room and flicked the switch on the wall, turning off the lights. Then she joined him at the window, parting the curtains and staring out. He felt her body stiffen as she saw the men too, then she was running from the window and snatching up the phone. Her finger jabbed at it three times and then she began talking.

Walking rose in alarm and crossed to the window, as she walked her foot caught the glass that had been resting on the floor beside her chair and it toppled over, spilling its rich red contents onto the carpet.

The Woman hung up the phone and ran to the kitchen, Marx followed and heard the rattle of items moving in a drawer as she jerked it open. She pulled out a long, gleaming knife and turned back to the hallway. Walking joined her and The Woman spoke to her quickly, her voice was strong and certain. The older woman nodded when she had finished and then climbed the stairs. Marx watched as she disappeared in the direction of Little One's room.

He stood at The Woman's feet and stared up at her, she looked determined and fierce. She would do anything to protect the girl, Marx knew, and he would too. Anything.

Two dark shapes appeared in the frosted glass of the door and then it began to shake in its frame as Loud and The Liar began pounding on it from the outside. Marx heard Loud shouting, his voice slurred and tired sounding but still full of the rage that characterised the man. The Woman called back to him, firmly but calmly and this triggered an angry, harsh explosion of words from him and another flurry of blows on the door. With each thump the door seemed to bulge inwards towards them. A photo of Little One that hung on the wall next to it jumped forward and fell to the floor, the glass fracturing over her smiling face. The flap of the letter box rattled with the blows, letting in short gusts of frigid air.

Marx and The Woman stood firm, watching and waiting.

And then suddenly it stopped. The banging on the door and the shouting ceased as suddenly as they had started and Marx heard a wailing electronic noise. The silhouettes of the two men were suddenly ringed in blue and then they vanished into the darkness.

Marx felt the tension go out of his body and saw the same thing happen to The Woman next to him. She turned and walked back to the kitchen returning the knife to the drawer. She called upstairs to Walking, who appeared with Little One by her side. The girl ran down to her mother and leapt into her arms. Marx could see the shining lines of moisture on her cheeks like bloodless claw marks.

A moment later there was a gentle knock at the door accompanied by the gentle sound of a woman's voice. Walking opened the door and Marx saw two of the blue clad people there, a man and a woman this time. They came in and talked to the women again. They wrote on their pads again and then they left. Again.

The Woman let them out of the house and then stood talking to them on the path for a moment. Their words sounded reassuring to Marx but he didn't know what weight they carried. Not much, he thought.

He walked back and forth on the damp grass in front of the house while they stood there, his eyes staring into the darkness, looking for Loud. He didn't see him, or the Liar, but as his eyes grew accustomed to the darkness he did see something else. That small square which The Liar had dropped. He walked to it and dipped his head to sniff it, catching the scent of the man and another rich, animal smell. He tapped it with his paw and it gave slightly. He had no idea what it was but wondered if it might help The Woman. He looked up and saw that the man and woman were walking away, back to their car with the blue lights on the top of it. The Woman was turning back towards the house and he meowed at her, she looked at him in surprise and then walked to him. When she saw the square at his feet she said something and then bent to pick it up. She looked at it and smiled, then picked him up too, pushing her face into his fur and kissing him.

Inside Walking and The Woman talked, they passed the square that Marx had found between them. They opened it and took out thin rectangles. Marx saw The Liar's face on one of them.

It seemed that Walking was trying to stop The Woman from doing something but Marx didn't know what. She was talking quickly and moving agitatedly, waving her thin arms. The Woman looked back at her calmly and shook her head. She spoke in a low, determined voice then she stood and walked to the kitchen. When she came back she was carrying the knife again, along with a tea towel which she was wrapping around it. She picked up the card with The Liar's face on it and walked to the door. Marx ran after her and when she opened the front door he ran through that.

The Woman stopped and looked at him and then just shook her head with a sad smile and walked to her car. Marx walked beside her and jumped into it when she opened the door.

He sat on the passenger seat as she drove, watching the lights of the other cars go by.

In time the car stopped. They were on a quiet street outside a dark house. The Woman pulled the card out of her pocket and examined it then looked at the house again. She grabbed the wrapped knife from the back seat and then climbed out of the car and knocked on the door of the house. The car door was still open and Marx sat watching her, ready to jump out if Loud or The Liar appeared. He had no idea where they were but he knew she had a purpose.

The door remained closed and after a time The Woman climbed back into the car and started the engine. She drove down the street a little and then turned it to face the house and stopped, turning the engine off and sitting in silence. Her hand found Marx in the darkness and she stroked him.

Marx was dozing when the stroking suddenly stopped. He opened his eyes and sat up, looking down the street and seeing Loud and The Liar walking towards the house. Both men moved with a clumsy looseness, The Liar staggering and hanging onto Loud to keep upright a couple of times. Marx didn't know what was wrong with them but at least they seemed less threatening.

When they reached the house, The Liar pulled out a key and opened the door. The two men walked in and the door closed. The Woman waited a short time time, stroking Marx in silence. He looked up at her and saw that she was crying, the tears running down her face and dripping from her chin. He lifted himself up and nuzzled her face, the moisture of the tears soaking into his fur. The Woman sucked in a deep breath and opened her door, climbing out of the car with the knife in her hand, still wrapped in the towel. Marx jumped after her and together they walked along the street.

She knocked loudly on the door of the house and then stepped to one side. It wasn't planned, but Marx somehow knew what she wanted him to do. He sat on the pavement and waited. The door opened and Loud appeared, scowling out into the night. Marx meowed once and the man looked down at him; then he ran, darting between Loud's legs and into the house. Loud growled and turned, stomping after him, as he did it The Woman slipped into the house.

Marx ran through into a room and saw The Liar stretched out on a sofa snoring, dead to the world. Loud ran in after him and lashed out with his foot, Marx dodged the kick and saw The Woman come in behind Loud. The man was already unsteady on his feet and the kick pushed him further off balance. Turning slightly as she ran, still clasping the knife, The Woman slammed her shoulder into Loud's back and sent him flying. He stumbled forward, his knee collided with a low table and he fell over it, crashing to the ground next to the sleeping Liar who didn't even stir. The woman jumped onto his back immediately, sitting on him, her two legs pinning his shoulders to the floor. She was much smaller than him but he was dazed from the fall and for now at least she had the upper hand.

Marx watched as she unwrapped the knife and swung it in front of Loud's face so he could see it. The cat didn't know what her intentions were, if she was here to kill the man who had terrorised her and her child, or if she merely intended to warn him off, to prove to him that he was as vulnerable as she was. She spoke to him in that steady, firm voice of hers, still sitting astride him, the long knife clasped in her hand.

Marx saw the man's muscles tense and knew suddenly that he was not as weak as he appeared. With a roar Loud pushed himself upwards, trying to throw The Woman off his back, with his hands flat on the ground he lifted their combined weight with deliberate strength. Marx knew the woman could stop it with one stab of the knife but she didn't, instead a look of fear and desperation came across her face. Marx did the only thing he could, he jumped forward at Loud. The man's sweating, grimacing face was level with Marx's and he swung at it, swiping his claws across Loud's eyes. They blinked shut instinctively a split second before the sharp points met flesh but Marx still did some damage, his claws catching and ripping the thin skin of the man's left eyelid. Marx saw a bead of blood blossom there and then fall to the ground as he swung again. His second strike worsened the damage and Loud yelled at him, droplets of saliva spraying from his mouth and landing on the cat's fur.

Loud relaxed his arms and let his body fall to the ground with a bang, then lashed out with one big hand, grabbing for Marx. The cat jumped back and then swiped at the hand for good measure.

Loud started shouting then, his anger directed at The Woman. His words were short and harsh like jabbing punches and they were relentless. Marx didn't know what he said but he saw a change come over The Woman. Her resolve returned but there was something else there too. Marx watched her sitting astride Loud and knew in that moment that she meant to end him. Her face had changed and it looked like Loud's now, full of anger and spite. This wasn't the gentle person he knew who stroked him and scratched him and let him nuzzle her face. This was a monster. He remembered the sound of Loud's fists hitting her flesh. He saw the look of terror on Little One's face as Loud drove away with her and he knew why The Woman was doing this. He also knew it would change her, that if she took Loud's life she would become him. Even though she was doing it for a good reason it would be the end of her as surely as it was of him.

Marx knew then that he had to stop her. He leapt forward, landing on Loud's back in front of The Woman. His eyes met hers and he was terrified by the fury he saw there. He opened his mouth and let out a quiet meow, calling to the tender creature he knew was inside. The nurturer, the carer, the mother. As he watched her The Woman's eyes cleared and she let out a great sob. The knife fell from her hand and landed on the dirty carpet next to Loud. With a roar of triumph the man heaved himself up again and Marx saw The Woman rock in front of him. Soon, the cat thought, soon he will throw her off and then he will fall on her and no amount of meowing will stop him.

He jumped, flying over Loud's head and twisting in the air to face the man as he landed. Loud's head was craned back as he strained to throw The Woman off, the tendons and veins of his neck protruding like worms under his flesh. Marx swiped at him again and again, his class scratching the skin, tearing through it.

Loud didn't stop to reach for Marx this time, his rage and determination clouded his reason. The cat's sharp talons ripped through the layers of his skin again and again but Loud ignored them.

The Woman saw what the cat was doing and redoubled her efforts, clinging on the man with all her strength. Marx kept scratching, his target was criss-crossed with lacerations now, they were numerous but all too shallow.

Finally, with one massive heave, Loud toppled The Woman from his back and hauled himself upright. She landed with a thud on the carpet and lay still, Marx couldn't tell if she was unconscious or had just given up. Loud raised a hand to his bloody throat and stared down at the cat, his face a mask of rage. He lashed out with a foot and Marx jumped backwards out of range. Loud took an unsteady step forward, furious eyes focussed on Marx, and then suddenly he was falling forward. The cat saw The Woman's legs sweeping around, catching Loud's and tripping him. The man pitched forward, arms flailing desperately, his head struck the wooden arm of the sofa The Liar still drunkenly slept on. He collapsed to the ground, stunned, his back hitting the carpet and his head snapping back against it. Marx pounced, landing softly by him and examining him warily. The man's eyes were half open but glazed. In the bloody mess of Loud's throat, he could see it, the vein of life beating there. If I'm going to do it, I need to do it now, Marx thought. So he did.

His mouth found the vein and he bit down with all his strength, clamping his teeth into it and then twisting his head from side to side to tear it. He felt it stretch and then rip and a huge gout of blood erupted from Loud's jugular.

Marx leapt back and watched as the man's life bled out of him onto the dirty floor.

The Woman took him home and he let her wash him clean of the thick, stick blood and then he slept. The next morning she picked him up and held him so tightly it almost hurt. Her body rocking with sobs and it rocked his too.

When she put him down again he could see something different in the way she regarded him. Maybe she now saw in him the same violence that she had seen in Loud, the same violence he had seen momentarily in her eyes. He had managed to stop her tumbling into that abyss but no-one had stopped him.

That night when Little One went to bed he trotted up the stairs after her but The Woman intercepted him, scooping him up and carrying him back downstairs. Little One spoke in a complaining tone and her mother replied firmly. Marx knew then that the balance of his life had changed.

It was time to leave.

When Little One came down for breakfast the next morning, Marx nuzzled her affectionately and sat beneath her chair as she ate. When she stood by the door pulling her coat on he rubbed himself against her legs until she giggled and told him to stop. And when the door opened he darted through it and ran out into the cold.

He looked back once and saw the three of them staring after him open mouthed, Little One, Walking and The Woman.

And then he turned the corner and they were gone.

Eulogy

The woman stood and walked to the front of the chapel, age had robbed her of some of her strength, the weight of emotion she felt had taken even more.

A microphone on a stand waited for her, a dark vertical line in her vision like an arrow pointing to the heavens. She reached it, took a breath, and began to speak:

"All of you knew my sister, that's why you're here today. Most of you met Jean before she got cancer. Some of you knew her as a girl, you heard that twinkling laugh she had back then. We used to call her Tinkerbell after the fairy in Peter Pan and she loved that. Those people will have known her as a young woman too, and will have seen the strength and determination to succeed that shaped everything she did. Our father walked out when we were girls and left us with nothing. Mother had no qualifications and we struggled. Those years made Jean determined that she would never rely on a man and by golly she didn't. Her career was a source of enormous pride and satisfaction to her and to me. I could never have achieved what she did and I used to look at her and think she was unstoppable.

"The cancer stopped her though. Took all that strength and whittled it away until all she could do was fight to get through each day. Those of you who worked with her will know how much it hurt her to have to give up her job, but she did, she had to. I think that hurt her almost as much as the disease itself.

"A few of you only met her after she became ill and most of the people who fall into that category met her through treatment. She made some good friends there, wonderful friends, and I'm sad to say that some of those people aren't with us anymore either. Jean watched good friends die but she didn't let it frighten her. In her final last year she came to be at peace with the disease, I think. She knew the end was coming and she was ready for it. Still, I know she would have found it funny that it wasn't the cancer that got her in the end. The fire robbed the disease of that satisfaction."

The woman paused and looked at the faces in front of her. So many of them.

"You all knew Jean in different ways and you'll all have your own stories to tell of her. I look forward to hearing those later. There are so many stories I could tell you, I knew her for her whole life after all, and I really struggled to choose one for today. It's silly isn't it, fretting over something like this, and Jean would have told me off for it. I've decided I will tell you about the last thing Jean did, because I think it really sums up the person she was. It was brave and selfless, and whilst she will never know it, it was an act that made a difference to other people's lives.

"They told me that the fire spread quickly, through from the kitchen and up the stairs in a flash. The front and back doors were blocked by it almost immediately and Jean must have known that. She was trapped upstairs, able to call the fire brigade but not to get out. All she could do was wait. She was used to waiting of course, waiting for death.

"After they had put the fire out they told me that she must have opened the window of her bedroom, they found it like that, wide open and blowing in the breeze. I puzzled on that for a while, there was no way Jean would have had the strength to climb out of it, but in time I realised that's not why she did it.

"Our cat Marx was in the house with her, you see, and she opened the window to save him. Heaven knows what he must have thought when she picked him up and threw him out of it, but being a cat he survived. No-one knew it except Jean and I hope in her last moment that gave her some happiness. The real miracle of what she did only came later though.

"When they finished putting the fire out they found Jean, of course, and I'm afraid I didn't even think of poor Marx. But days later he came back. I don't know where he ran to when he left the house but I know he ended up with two people who needed him. Two people who have come to be almost like family to me in the short time I have known them.

"So, with death breathing down on her, Jean did something magical. She rescued Marx and he rescued them. That, ladies and gentlemen, was my sister."

A Note from the Author

'A Cat Called Hope' started as bit of a joke.

I began publishing my fiction early in 2012, most of my work falls into the crime and horror genres and fairly quickly friends and relatives started saying to me "Why don't you write anything nice". Now nice, to be perfectly honest, is not what my writing is about, so I was a little bit reluctant at first. After a while though I started thinking that it might be an interesting experiment, I tossed the idea around in my head for a while and landed on the idea of writing a cat story.

I seem to remember I got the opening written fairly quickly, up until the point when Walking throws poor startled Marx out of the window, and then the story languished. The beginning seemed to me to have the makings of a decent story, the pampered house cat thrust out into a hostile world, but I had nowhere to go with it. I desperately didn't want to write a 'Homeward Bound' style story of a plucky cat meeting other animals, I wanted to create something that felt real.

I'm not sure exactly where the Little One, Loud and The Woman came from, but once they had appeared in my imagination the rest of the story wrote itself.

I published the finished story without much expectation, none of my books to that point had sold many copies, but I had received the occasional kind review or comment by someone who had come across one of them. I realised fairly quickly that 'A Cat Called Hope' was a rather different beast. It went on sale on 22nd July and by the end of the month it had sold more copies than any of my other short stories. By the end of August it had almost matched the sales for my novel, 'Sunliner', which had been on sale since February. At the end of 2012 I had published 12 books. The sales for 'A Cat Called Hope' exceeded the other 11 put together.

What made me even happier were the reviews. Somehow I had created something which resonated with people in a way I had never expected. Not all the reviews have been good, I still remember the sinking of my heart when I read one particularly passionate one star diatribe, but the people who liked it REALLY liked it. As a writer to have someone comment that your book has reduced them to tears is a pretty amazing thing.

So, in 2013 I resolved to write a sequel. As with the first book it was slow going and I ended up putting it to one side whilst I worked on my second novel, 'One Night'.

Eventually 'A Cat Called Hope Returns' was finished and I published it in March. Gratifyingly, people seemed to like it just as much as the first book and some even asked for another. I started thinking about possible plots and hit a brick wall. Loud had been defeated at the end of the first story and then come back again in the second only to be beaten again. I remembered the cartoons I'd watched as a kid, He-Man and Thundercats and the like, where the heroes beat the villains at the end of each episode but never in a way final enough for them not to return the following week. I didn't want the 'Cat Called Hope' books to fall into this trap.

The more I thought it through the more I realised that I needed to bring things to a logical conclusion and so the concept of 'The Final Chapter' was born. I wanted to write a story that wrapped up the tale of The Woman, Walking and Little One but which also freed Marx to go on further adventures.

This was the easiest book in the series to write by far and as I wrote it I came to realise that in fact the stories contain absolutely everything I want to write about. There is heroism, there is passion, there is darkness and there is excitement. Marx, it seems to me, is a hero from the same mould as Jack Bauer from '24' and Rick Grimes from 'The Walking Dead'. He always does what he feels is right no matter what the danger to himself or the sacrifice he has to make, this is true no more so than in the end of the third book.

Once I'd finished writing 'The Final Chapter', I realised it made sense to publish a collected edition. I think the stories work best together, with a logical flow to them that makes Marx's tale into a novella rather than three separate short stories. I wanted to give anyone kind enough to purchase the complete edition a little something extra, so I wrote the short piece 'Eulogy' to include in it. The two most common questions I have had from readers on the series are: "Did Sleeping die?" and "What was the nature of Walking and Sleeping's relationship?" Hopefully 'Eulogy' answers both of those queries.

If you've got this far I'd like to thank you for going on this journey with me and Marx and for taking the time to read my rambling thoughts on the books. I hope you enjoy them and that you'll go on a few more adventures with the two of us.

Oliver Clarke

Sussex, September 2013

Also by Oliver Clarke

One Night – a romantic thriller

He was on the run from death, she was on the run from life. Would one night together be enough?

Joel had no reason to live, he just didn't want to die. Running from a gang of vicious criminals who are out for his blood he arrives in wintry Southend with no plan beyond staying alive long enough to make one.

Eve is alone, tortured by her past and dreading a future of nothingness. When she meets Joel all she wants is a good time. The last thing she expects is that she'll end up running for her life and falling in love with a man who will lead her to uncover truths about her own past that will shake her soul.

Set in a single night, One Night is the gripping story of two people finding each other and the strength to deal with the demons in their pasts. Thrilling, romantic and sensual it will move and excite you and live with you long after the last page.

Printed in Great Britain
by Amazon.co.uk, Ltd.,
Marston Gate.